Winter Is

Ann Dixon

Illustrated by Mindy Dwyer

ALASKA NORTHWEST BOOKS™

The name Alaska Northwest Books and the caribou logo are trademarks of
Graphic Arts Center Publishing Company.

Library of Congress Cataloging-in-Publication Data
Dixon, Ann.
    Winter is / Ann Dixon ; illustrated by Mindy Dwyer.
        p. cm.
    Summary: A boy and girl describe winter and the wonderful activities of that season,
but also look forward to summer.
    ISBN 0-88240-543-8 — ISBN 0-88240-544-6 (pbk.)
    [1. Winter—Fiction. 2. Stories in rhyme.] I. Dwyer, Mindy, 1957– ill. II. Title.

PZ8.3.D6248 Wi 2002
[E]—dc21

2002023340

Alaska Northwest Books™
An imprint of Graphic Arts Center Publishing Company
P.O. Box 10306, Portland, Oregon 97296-0306
503-226-2402
www.gacpc.com

President/Publisher: Charles M. Hopkins
Associate Publisher: Douglas A. Pfeiffer
Editorial Staff: Timothy W. Frew, Ellen Harkins Wheat, Tricia Brown, Jean Andrews,
    Kathy Matthews, Jean Bond-Slaughter
Production Staff: Richard L. Owsiany, Susan Dupere
Book and cover design: Andrea L. Boven / Boven Design Studio, Inc.

Printed in Singapore

Winter is coming and I can't wait!

*I*ce creaks and groans,
freezing thick on the lake.
How long will it be
till the ice doesn't break?

At last! We can skate and glide.

Now winter is here,
numbing noses and toes.
On porch doors and windows
a frost garden grows.

Winter is white.
Sparkling snow piles up high.
We shovel a rooftop.
Now look at us fly!

In fluffy snow pillows we land.

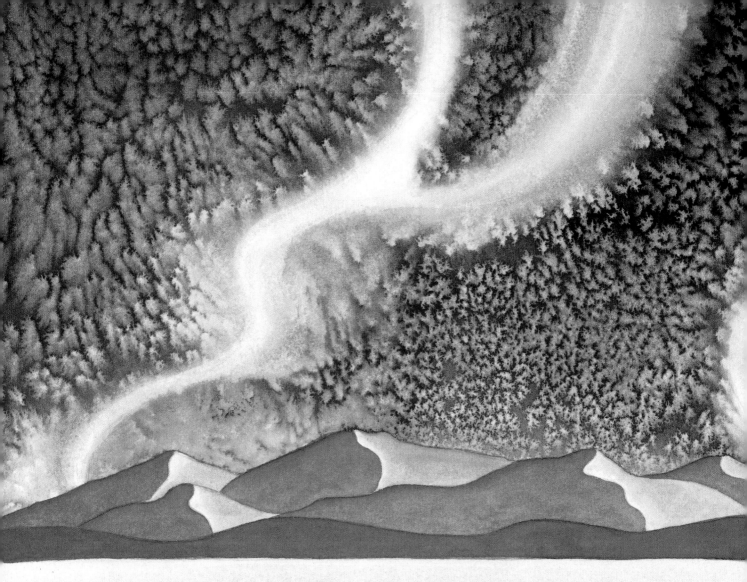

$\mathcal{W}$inter is black,
spilling night into day.
We watch northern lights
start to flicker and sway.

They swirl like bright, crazy dancers.

*W*inter is *cold*,
sending shivers down deep.
In thick, furry coats
the wild animals sleep.

Shhh! Don't wake them, please!

*W*inter is dark,
making shadows all 'round.
Our lantern beam leaps
as we mush homeward bound.

What a bouncing trail to follow!

Winter is light,
bringing holiday cheer.
Through long, cozy nights
bulbs and candles shine clear.

Our dreams fill with toys,
treats, and treasures.

Winter is bright.
Stepping softly we prowl.
We're watching and listening
for moose, fox, and owl.

Moonbeams shimmer around us.

Late winter is warm,
melting hills in the sun.
We throw off our coats
for another sled run.

Back down we swoosh and we slide.

Winter is long.
Thawing snow *drip drip drips.*
We step off the path
and sink up to our hips!

Laughing, we empty our boots.

*N*ow winter is gone,
trailing patches of snow.
Through thickets of willow,
young moose say "hello."

We call, but they run to their mother.

At last the ice melts.
Landing ducks splash the lake.
Our footsteps ooze mud.
Budding trees are awake.

Look! The world is light, leafy green.

Summer is coming and I can't wait!

To my parents, Barbara Mae Cook Dixon (1927–1994) and David Sherman Dixon (1926–2001). —AD

For all of my loved ones in Alaska. —MD